CHAPTER ONE Men at War

In this first poem I attempt to recreate the atmosphere of how I think it would have been in England in1914, there was an air of excitement among the younger men who rushed to join up in case they should miss the great adventure, Married men just thought it their duty, but all thought it would all be over for Christmas - if only they had known.

Leaving Home

The Salvation Army band played
as the rain began to cascade,
people passing could not be swayed
to join the Captain as he prayed.

Two children stood idly around,
the look on their faces profound,
they seemed hypnotised by the sound,
their holey shoes scraping the ground.

I tarried there at my front door
kissed my weeping wife once more,
heard the home crowd at the Albion roar,
grabbed my bags and headed off to war.

The cobbled streets were awash
with newspapers about the Bosche,
Lord Kitchener failed to whitewash--
the fear hid behind his moustache.

Turned my collar to cold and damp,
as I walked beneath the gas lamp,
on my way to the army camp,
head held high I charged up the ramp.

In the inspection room, I waited,
on getting through I concentrated,
hoping I'd be A1 rated
and all my dreams not be deflated.

The ambience told its own tale,
as Captain said stand on the scale,
although quite thin and very frail,
I had to pass - just couldn't fail.

So that was it! No fear or fuss,
there's nothing more left to discuss,
my worries were all superfluous--
and I'd be back home for Christmas!

This poem is about one of the most controversial stories of WW1, the story of how a sudden truce came about in the trenches on Christmas morning, I have taken my words from a true story of a soldier who was actually there on the day, the only controversial story of what really happened that day was the football match, but even so - that may have been true.

'StilleNacht, (Silent Night)'

It was cold that grey Christmas in the trench,
Fresh snow had fallen the previous night,
But not even the cold could mask the stench,
of the gangrene caused by severe frostbite,
the continuous sniping without respite.

Yet that Christmas eve in nineteen fourteen,
An unofficial spontaneous truce,
A reprieve from the shelling that had been,
Adjournment of the terrible abuse,
fleeting freedom from the tightening noose.

We had all received packages of food,
really lifting the spirits of each side,
The torrential day's rain had now subdued,
Brave men who were heroes sat misty eyed,
wondering how war had been glorified.

'May God protect you and bring you back home'
Princess Mary engraved on a metal case,
Tobacco and sweets under a lid of chrome,
Butterscotch and chocs put smiles on our face,
gifts from back home one could never replace.

The Germans wanted peace, made the first move,
by sending a cake across to our line,
How could we weary soldiers disapprove,
We sent them tobacco, said that was fine,
the thought of peace sent shivers down my spine,

'It'll be over by Christmas' we were told,
Could this be the start of peace in our time,
We were now broken men who once were bold,
Old men at twenty, last year, in our prime,
put in ready made graves, covered in grime.

Christmas goodwill spread twenty seven miles,
Along the trenches it travelled so fast,
Hell holes now filled with happiness and smiles,

Each man wondering, how long would it last,
but for now a peace, a calm unsurpassed.

Then we all heard it, that sound from afar,
Germans singing StilleNacht (Silent Night)
Up in the sky a bright shining star,
shone on No man's land, setting alight
the destruction, mayhem, remains of the fight.

Next day at eight thirty, winter sun rose,
Four German men appeared on No man's land,
Shouting across, 'We are friends, not your foes,
we wanted to come to shake your hand'
men climbed out of trenches, though it was banned.

A soldier offered his hand, I held out mine
We looked at each other, doubting, unsure,
I gave him a cigarette, a Wills woodbine,
He gave me a drink, first taste of liqueur,
although my enemy, I still felt secure.

Within half an hour hundreds of men,
Sharing their photos, talked like old friends,
Souvenirs swapped and exchanged again,
Insults given out, not meant to offend
thousands of men, wished the day wouldn't end.

Way down the line a football match was played,
so I heard later, that cold Christmas night,
when back to the trenches our way we made,
To my new German friend, I bid goodnight,
for tomorrow we must resume the fight.

Come the morning we would fire from afar
but it was nice just to show how human we are!

---

*Conditions in the trenches were dire, men were consistently up to
their knees in mud and foul blood filled water, one of the worst
threats was the enemy sniper, if a soldier showed just the top of his
head he was a dead man. Whilst soldiers on both sides lived in this
hell some of the high ranks enjoyed a life of luxury in Chateaus well
away from the noise and the stench.*

A last smoke

I do not recognise my friend,
as I sit with him to the end,
This face I'd known from boy to man,

split open like a corned beef can.

How can my God allow this hell?
of sniper's gun - enemy shell,
A battleground where nothing's gained,
bullet and bombs ...a war sustained!

The Generals... they hide and cower,
sitting in their ivory towers,
Then order thousands o'er the top,
if you don't go you're for the chop.

Last week we formed a firing squad,
we shot a lad... poor frightened sod!
No one knew who had the bullet,
finger on the trigger, pull it.

That boy whose feeble mind was locked,
was not a coward - just shell shocked,
But they shot the bugger anyway,
on a cold and grey November day.

And now I'm sat here with my chum.
he says his legs are going numb,
I hold a Woodbine to his mouth,
the bullets flying north and south.

I hear a gurgle from his throat,
in that dark place - wet and remote,
Then crimson from his lips it fell,
and to my friend... I bid farewell.

_A millions horses and mules were mobilised during WW1, over
400,000 were killed, and another 400,000 injured beyond help, only
170,000 made it through and most of these could not be shipped
back home after the war, the cost was far too expensive. This poem
tells of the love and understanding between a soldier and his horse._

War Horse

Goodbye old friend, you've served me well;
you did your job throughout this hell.
Exhausted - now you're lying here;
within your eyes I see the fear.

My pal is calling...let him go,
he'll never learn, he'll never know
how dire it is to lose a friend,

but I'll stay with you to the end.

And if the Hun should come before
you've breathed your last in this damn war,
then, so be it, I'll die with you,
for loyal friends must see it through

until the end, when we'll be seen
as one - once more on England's green
and pleasant land for which we fought,
to plough God's fields as we were taught.

I hear the bullets whizzing by,
the screaming men, the battle cry.
You lift your head to shield my heart,
and bullets tear your neck apart.

I hold you tight with bloodied hand,
I try to rise, I try to stand.
I feel the shrapnel from the shell--
Goodbye old friend, you served me well

Whilst soldiers or scouts were on patrol they would often come
across an unknown grave with perhaps a helmet placed on the top
of a rusting Enfield rifle, this is the story of one such scout.

An Unknown Soldier

While on patrol close by a rill,
I spied a cross upon a hill,
No name was written on that cross,
No one was left to mourn his loss.

I felt a peace sweep over me,
Where once had been a killing spree,
I stood.. I stared - my gun in hand,
Upon that God-forsaken land.

'My friend although you're lying here,
Your enemy you did not fear,
With rustic cross to mark your space,
Will anyone recall your face?.

I know it's in this place you stood,
And gave your life for truth and good,
For poppies grow from your spilt blood,
Now rising from the scarlet mud.

Fear not my friend, 'twas not in vain,
For peace will come to reign again',
I knelt and bowed my head in prayer,
For unknown soldier buried there.

My bayonet worn at my side,
I used to carve these words with pride,
'A brave man lies beneath this sod'
An Unknown soldier... known to God'.

---

*Gas was the soldiers worst enemy, it started with the French in 1914
using mild irritants such as tear gas, the Germans retaliated with
more disabling types of gas, By 1916 gas designed to kill within 24
hours was being used, an old soldier would keep his mask close but
raw recruits - though warned - were a little more reckless.*

Gas!

Conditions were perfect for an enemy attack,
I rummaged for a ciggy inside my backpack.
I sat on the fire step - smoking Woodbine I'd found,
Feeling nice and relaxed with my putees unwound.

The lad on the periscope was new to the game;
His christening in trenches was, thankfully, tame.
He shouted, "Hey, sergeant, this is really profound,
There's a yellow green cloud rolling over the ground."

Grabbing my bayonet, I banged on a spent shell.
Some other trenchers raised the alarm as well,
With less than twenty seconds before it arrived.
It's only the quickest and smartest that survived.

I picked up my gas mask, pulled it over my head.
The lad on the periscope was already dead!
I saw him sink to the mud, clutching his throat-
An awful way to die in a place so remote.

Pandemonium reigned for a while in our trench.
We fixed our bayonets with a twist and a wrench.
More new men lined the fire step - took up the slack,
Crouching -waiting for the imminent attack.

The company mascot lay muddied and froze;
His saturated paws were covering his nose.
The animals suffered ... the horse and the mule;
All of the rats died adding to the cesspool!

Then, over they came, their bayonets glistening;
I prayed to dear God...He must have been listening...
They came in full force but we repelled the attack;
We were all exhausted, but we turned them back.

My head seemed to burst - I heard a crack in my ear.
The trench turned to a snake, my vision was unclear.
My mask was leaking - pins and needles everywhere;
I felt myself drifting and lost consciousness there.

I awoke with a start as fresh air filled my throat,
As I lay on a stretcher, beneath a great coat,
Examining my mask - a bullet had gone through:
Gas had penetrated but I hadn't a clue.

The damage to my lungs terminated my fight;
I was honourably discharged...went home to write.
This was supposed to be the war to end all war,
But, twenty years later, we had to face more!

During WW1 as I said earlier Horses were used extensively for moving goods, cannons etc, dogs were also used for getting messages to headquarters along with trained pigeons. without these courageous animals many more men would have died.

The Killing Fields

The ghosts of men in killing fields,
Bright red poppies are all it yields,
Born from the blood of those who fell,
From sniper's gun and cannon shell.

The war horse standing tall and proud,
Now dead in battlefields he ploughed,
Buried alive upon the Somme
and never knowing who had won.

The German Shepherd sitting there,
Is that uncanny...? I don't care!
Those dogs saved many English lives,
and sent men home to mums and wives.

The cross of white just says it all,
Reminding man of his shortfall,
For when they fight and bullets fly,
Then man will surely have to die.

Man, dog or horse, whichever it be,
Gave of their lives so we walk free,
This solemn picture now long gone,
Reminds us we should live... as one!

For all the tears that mothers cried,
For all those brave men who have died,
For that old soldier stood outside-
Who sold you a poppy, wear it with pride

---

*The **Battle of Vimy Ridge** was a military engagement fought primarily as part of the Battle of Arras, in the Nor-Pas-de-Calaise region of France, during the war, The main combatants were the four divisions of the Canadian Corps in the First army, against three divisions of the German 6th Army. The battle, which took place from 9 to 12 April 1917, was part of the opening phase of the Battle of Arras, the first attack of the Nivelle Offensive, intended to attract German reserves from the French front.*

The Battle of Vimy Ridge.

The History

One hundred years ago today
On Easter Monday far away
Twenty thousand soldiers brave
Prepared themselves for early grave
Canadians each and every one
Someone's husband, someone's son
Got ready for a sustained attack
So many of them would not come back.

Vimy ridge in Northern France
Prevented any new advance
Allied attempts in earlier years
Left many mothers wiping their tears
Then late in Autumn-nineteen sixteen
Four divisions of Corps were seen
First time together as a nation
Canadians all, in one formation.

Those fearless men so full of courage
Were sent to attack Vimy ridge
Preparations – so extensive
Left them feeling oh so pensive
Those Germans dug in, deep on high
Behind their guns would defy
Anyone to climb that hill
And any who tried they would surely kill.

Canadian preparation

Winter was spent strengthening lines
Digging tunnels and underground mines
A lighted system and railway track
Carried explosives for the attack
Well beneath the German trench
Were water lines ready to quench
The dry throats of those thirsty men
Some would not see daylight again.

Allies shelled them with a barrage
Rained shells on them before the charge
For one whole week one million shells
Would fall on Germans in that hell
Military aircraft of the day
Swept observation balloons away
Germans who'd seen many rougher things
Named it their 'Week of suffering'

The Battle

An allied barrage timed to the minute
Allowed protection of those behind it
As it moved on the Hun were surprised
Leaving their bunkers – uncompromised
To see Canadians with their guns
Shouting hands up to the frightened Hun
So they advanced and by noon next day
Hill one four five was taken away.

Two days later the battle was won
Germans withdrew, or lay down their gun
But victory came at a cost
Three thousand six hundred were lost
Ten thousand wounded, such a great loss
Four men earned the Victoria cross
Those brave Canadians would lose many more
Before the end of that Bloody war.

The Legacy

Today they have their monument
Where many a quiet moment is spent
Looking over green countryside
Where so many young – fought and died
A legacy from a grateful France
To all those lads that took their chance
Canadians each and every one
Someone's husband, Someone's son.

It was not unusual for soldiers to be sent back home on a few days leave from the horror of the trenches on the Somme, it was also not unusual for young men not yet of age for war to have white feathers pressed into their hand by young smiling ladies, I wrote this poem to show just how easy it was to make a mistake in wartime.

Silent witness

Came home from Ypres knocked on the door
Down beaten, dishevelled, but they knew the score,
Mum cuddled me close when she heard my voice
I told her my uniform's crawling with lice.

She took a step back and said 'it's alright,
I'll get them boiled up, wear civvies tonight,
So, out came the tin bath, hard brush and all
The suit from the wardrobe reeked of mothballs.

They pressed me with questions, was it as bad
As they'd heard off the next door neighbours lad,
I didn't say much, said it wasn't very nice
Mum knew I was lying from the quake in my voice.

Father decided we'd all have a ball
We went to a show down the Music hall,
Back in my civvies I felt really grand
Then a girl pressed a white feather into my hand.

I felt so embarrassed, I wished I had died!
Civilian clothes had battered my pride,
If she'd only known what I had been through
But I remained silent and didn't argue.

Then, in the foyer, an officer said
'You should be in uniform – hold up your head!'
He called me a coward, a maggot, a worm
His words were hurtful, making me squirm.

My parents had disappeared into the crowd
I'd killed for my country – but I wasn't proud,
I looked at their faces, pompous and smug
Dress in my civvies I felt like a thug!

I stormed out of the hall, walked home alone
When suddenly, I was hit by a stone,
A group of young kids shouted 'Coward' at me
Went running away down a dark alley.

Soldiers in uniform spat at my feet
Old people snubbed me on my own street,
Had I changed so much, that they couldn't see
How hard I had fought to keep them free.

I arrived home, put my uniform on
returned to the hall – passed everyone,
Including the kids who'd thrown that stone
got smiles from the old people going home.

The girl with the feather stood on the street
I held out my hand as if to greet,
Then pressed the white feather back into her hand
the shock on her face was really quite grand.

I saw that officer stood on the path
His laughter and gaiety filled me with wrath,
I crossed the road told him what I thought
about the commission he'd probably bought.

Asked him if he'd ever been to war
Did he know, what we were fighting for,
Not to be ridiculed by lesser men
but so we could all have our freedom again.

I walked away having stated my cause
I could hear behind me rapturous applause,
There are no truer words spoken than
the words of Shakespeare,' Clothes make the man'

Next day I returned – back to the mayhem
Where men are men, not so quick to condemn.
It wasn't the outcome I would prefer
But at least I knew who my enemy were!

When new recruits were being taken to new positions they would often have to make way for refugees fleeing from their homes and towns.

The Refugees (No escape)

We passed them as we marched away
Defenceless, ragged from the fray,
Pitiful beings on the road
Upon their backs a heavy load,
Their faces glowing in retreat
From burning buildings on the street,
Women, children, priests and nuns

Unfazed by the booming guns,
They stumbled by, breaking our hearts
Pushing prams and pulling carts,
With all their worldly goods on board
Not just possession – memories stored,
Of life long gone, a life of peace
Family snaps on mantle-piece,
The setting sun at close of day
In fields where now dead bodies lay,
Would be their new home overnight
Until next day at early light,
Weary, shuffling endless column
Unwashed children looking solemn,
Trudging on their trips unplanned
Toward another war torn land.

This poem is an attempt to show the horrors of war from the viewpoint of a soldier.

The Valiant

No trees remain on barren land
where valiant soldiers made their stand.
Those muddied craters in the ground
where bodies lie - now void of sound.

The stench of death is everywhere,
a smell of gas that fills the air.
Those young men all deceived - abused,
who lie beside grenade's unused-

once walked o'er grass with wives, girlfriends,
said 'Home for Christmas when it ends'--
no longer have the voice to talk,
no longer have the legs to walk.

A picture of a sweetheart's face
in bloodied hand - looks out of place.
The sadness shows in staring eyes...
no time for kisses or goodbyes.

Captain's research all slipshod,
now leads his men toward their God,
To be with Him, to take His hands
those brave lads killed in foreign lands.

Those mothers' sons - though valiant all
had wished they'd never heard the call,

They hadn't known such grief, such pain,
but soon their sons would fight again!

Scouts in WW1 were independent units of about six men, they weren't subject to the same routine as other men, the stress of their work would mean that they set up their own camps and drew their own rations, their work was very dangerous so they would do three days and nights in the field and then take three days well earned rest.

The Scout.

The year was nineteen seventeen
when new recruits joined our platoon,
Their faces shocked at what they'd seen
for some- the war had come too soon.
But this new blood and old would weld
together as the wounded men
returned to posts some once had held
still wondering why, where and when.

The end of May was wonderful
Behind the lines the ruins were hid,
By tall grass – colourful – not dull
Garden flowers which someone did
nurture so lovingly and tend,
as wild ones all along the wall
seeded themselves once more to blend
Before we came and spoiled it all.

Everywhere the waste of war
was softened by prolific surge,
of unchecked crops which now did soar
from blood soaked soil they did emerge.
Within a stone's throw of the guns
the mating birds would build their nest,
sitting – chirping, on the cannons
their joyful songs were surely blest.

By nightfall we had reached the place
a thousand yards from German lines,
The shelling here at gentler pace
where road and village intertwine,
An oasis in landscape of mud
where we could rest and be at peace,
Deep inside a dense deep wood
we'd wait for daylight to decrease.

We always worked in groups of three
So one would stay behind in camp,
He'd stay preparing food and tea
for our return in cold and damp.
Then, under cover of black night
we'd head toward the German lines,
Watching everything in sight
listening for the danger signs.

All I.D was left behind
no discs or letters should death loom,
No information could they find
if trench became our catacomb,
No steel helmets on our head
in case it clanged against our gun,
We wore a forage cap instead
and a bandolier for the hun.

One black night whilst on patrol
the moon was hid by thick grey cloud,
Through No Man's land and near our goal
when we heard voices talking loud,
We lay quite still upon wet ground
as Germans passed us within yards,
They walked quite freely homeward bound
and didn't bother with rear guards.

When suddenly a Verey light
lit up the sky and all around.
Everything was snowy white
even the mud upon the ground,

Machine gun fire scoured the hill,
on which we hid away from view,
Our men's bullets trying to kill
the Germans and attempted coup.

As daylight dawned things became hushed
we had been on that hill all night.
We needed to go but wouldn't be rushed
until the time became right,
We slowly crept back to our base
hidden deep within the wood,
We could leave. have a change of pace
but we wouldn't although we should.

Men thought our job a dangerous one
our workplace – in No Man's Land.
But we drew and cooked our own ration
dismissed fatigues out of hand,

Each forth day was a day of rest
spent in an observation post,
Better than sat in a trench so stressed
with death on your mind uppermost.

We scouts survived – no man was lost
out there on Menin road Ridge,
Although this war came at a cost
to millions held hostage,
The Menin road where we now stood
and the battle yet to come,
Was nothing but a river of mud
As we trudged our way back home.

A lot of soldiers throughout the war suffered from shellshock, the constant barrage of shells, the snipers and the general conditions would cause even the most level headed man to lose control.

A Soldiers prayer

Woke with a start - unsettled sleep,
the morning light began to creep,
tired and weary familiar men,
waiting for war to start again.

A young man stumbled, as though blind,
like some poor wretch who'd lost his mind,
Clutching a Bible in his hand,
stared bleakly out to no man's land.

I sat beside him in that trench,
the pouring rain began to drench,
it almost washed his soul away,
I watched him as he knelt to pray.

'Abide with me today dear Lord,
give me the strength to wield my sword,
as new day dawns the guns may cease,
I'm grateful for the calm and peace'.

The soldier stood, looked to his God,
and said, 'Dear Lord this path I've trod,
was not the way of life I chose...
to kill mankind, although my foes.

Yes, I was angry with my foe,
my hate was strong, my wrath did grow,

until I saw those sons so brave,
lying face down in shallow grave.

If I should fall in foreign land,
then come to me, reach for my hand,
and take me to a better place,
that I might look upon your face.

And so dear Lord - to you I pray,
don't let this be our judgement day,
but bring us love and peace instead...
let England mourn - bury her dead.'

I never saw that lad again,
I looked for him but searched in vain,
for we were all caught on the hop
and then were ordered o'er the top!

Then five years on - in civvy street,
one day by chance I got to meet,
the soldier who had prayed that day,
one of the few who got away.

Went to the cafe, ordered tea,
he said how he remembered me,
took off his coat, revealed much more,
of the Vicar's collar that he wore.

---

*Most men wrote home at one time or another, it broke the
boredom of the trenches, married soldiers wrote home to their
wives, some to their girlfriends, but the majority of young single
recruits sent letters back home to their mothers, letters such as
this--*

A Letter Home

'Dear mother, I'll see you again',
He wrote these words while wracked with pain,
Up to his waist in muck and mud,
Hole in his stomach -- oozing blood.

At just eighteen he took the shilling,
Spirit strong and very willing,
The town had naught to offer him,
Families starved, times were grim.

Shook Granddad's hand, felt like a man,
He'd fought his war in the Sudan,
Kissed mother's cheek at the front door,
And marched away to glorious war.

But first he must learn how to fight...
Learn what was wrong and what was right,
At barracks he would make new friends,
Experience pays dividends!

He learned to stand erect and tall,
Fight to the end - to kill not brawl,
To march so proudly around the square,
He wished his dad could see him there!

Just six months later on the Somme,
Stray shrapnel from a German bomb,
Had left him with a gaping hole...
And fear of death within his soul.

With bloodied hand he held the pen,
Began to write 'See you again,
I love you mother - truly care,
Look to your side and I'll be there.'

His pen and hand slipped into mud,
He died alone where he once stood,

Learning to march stood him in stead..
On Heaven's stairs he joined the dead!

On the 11th of November at 11.00am the war with Germany officially ended, this is my take on how I thought those soldiers would think, I hope I've got it right.

The end of War

I recall that day - the eleventh of November,
We were still fighting hard, that's what I remember,
Our men were still dying we knew nothing of peace,
that within a few hours this damn war would cease.

Pinned down by machine guns and close to a village,
one lone house remained, unaffected by pillage.
When a runner brought news it came as a shock,
that the war would be ended at eleven o clock.

At precisely eleven the bullets just stopped,
then from enemy trenches, an officer popped,
He took off his helmet and bowed low to our troops,
Lined up his tired men - marched away to great whoops.

There was no sense of vengeance , no need to berate,
Though... temptation to shoot them was still very great,
we were just very grateful for the little we'd got-
Like standing up straight without getting shot.

It was pure anti-climax, no emotion remained,
four horrifying years and little was gained,
The Allies had victory but at a great cost,
I thought of my comrades - good friends I had lost.

We were all too exhausted, too tired to enjoy,
awaited our orders to perhaps redeploy,
No cheering - no singing, no alcohol at all,
But a time to be thankful - we'd not heard God's call.

---

*In 1918 when men came home from the war they were
different, the horrors of the trenches had changed their looks,
their moods and their manner, some were coming home to
children they had hardly seen, this poem is my take on how I
thought a wife would react when her husband returned.*

Coming home

He finally came back to me, but not the man I married,
He brought with him despair so grim, as at the door he tarried,
Seemed weather beaten... hadn't eaten, his face both glum and harried,
He looked so tired, his eyes expired - from memories he carried.

He sat right down, his face a frown, and not a word was spoken,

Stared at the fire, his gaze so dire, his mind empty and broken,
That frightened man reached for my hand, his love was but a token,
A brave young man who'd made a stand, but senses now awoken.

What happened to the man I knew, where had his spirit gone?
Left on the brink among the stink of trenches on the Somme,
He yells in sleep from slumber deep, 'Come on my boys - come on,
Don't you dare stop we're o'er the top when whistle blows anon.'

He's grown a beard...this man now feared, his hair's in need of comb,
His haunted face deserves no place, in this our loving home.
I tried to speak, his eyes were bleak, back to the war they'd roam,
His mind was vexed just as complex as any honeycomb.

This bloody war though now no more, yet memories remain,
Man's mighty sword now not so broad - worn down by death and pain,
In God we trust...we surely must, or what would be the gain?
I look to Bill and with man's will, this can't occur again!

CHAPTER TWO The Aftermath

Today we look after our old soldiers, but it wasn't always like that, and even now some slip the net, with this poem I look at just one of those men, during the eighties we had a dog eat dog environment in this country, the rich got richer and the poor got poorer, this poem is set in that era.

Forgotten Soldier

All the world he ever knew is gone
Damp bedsit keeps him from the cold
He hardly sees the sun that shone
Old soldier once so brave, so bold

For king and country he once served
With Lee Enfield, post is manned
The medals, now long gone deserved
For a few pounds, pressed in shaky hand

Meagre pension spent on food and rent
A few bob left for electric fire
Yet for his life he does not lament
Although his life at times is dire

The kettle whistles on an old camp stove
Tea bag meets mug for the third time
hand around handle donning fingerless glove
That hides the sores amongst the grime

Grey old eyes stare over steaming cup
Clutched with both hands for the heat
Sore chapped lips take another sup
Of the tea, milkless and unsweet

Old washstand in the corner stays
Though not used for three weeks and a half
No water in the house for days
Since turned off by waterboard staff

Yet water runs down blistered walls
And gathers on top of the skirting
Sad eyes slowly close, his mind recalls
World war one and all it's hurting

He's suddenly back in the trenches
Full of friends so tired, so brave
Knee deep in the mud, the blood, the stench
Knee deep in a ready made grave

Down steep narrow steps into muck and mire
Along splintered duckboards, into the dugout
Safety at last from the line of fire
Respite from the battle until the next bout

One precious hour of sleep in a bunk
Beneath low ceiling, dull flickering light
Head in a spin as though punch drunk
One precious hour before return to the fight

Although exhausted, sleep would not come
Was that a rat that ran over the bed
Head still banging like a drum
What would he give for a dry bedspread

All too soon he returns to the fray
Across rat eaten boards above the mud
German machine guns begin to spray
And their artillery barrage lands with a thud

German bullets whistle over their heads
In the hellish earthquake of Passchendaele
The stench of corpses, the limbless dead
As the enemy again begin to assail

Shell craters full of bloodstained water
The intolerable horror returned to his mind

Millions of men brought to senseless slaughter
Where explosions and screams together bind

In the trenches death and devastation brewing
Never ending screams and howls through the night
One young soldier his last breath spewing
As chaplain gives him last rites

Suddenly a deadly silence descended
The Captain immaculate, from dugout came
German barrage temporarily suspended
Leaving only the cries of the wounded and lame

They knew from his sad look, they were over the top
Which caused adrenaline and fear to flow
But in that dank place they would rather stop
For out there were the deadly foe

The whistles blew along the salient
Young men clambered out to their death
The enemy opened fire all along the front
And hundreds drew their last breath

Come on brave lads' the Captain yelled
As a bullet slammed into his chest
Into the mud that brave man was felled
Alongside others who had failed the test

Like lambs to the slaughter the young men ran
Hindered by barbed wire and mud
Into the hell of no mans land
But most just cut down where they stood

The old soldier woke as memories stirred
Those memories he'd held for sixty years
Yet not once had he ever spoken a word
Though many times eyes had filled with tears

A home fit for heroes was promised to all
But they returned to slums and no work
Four years earlier they heeded Kitcheners call
And not one would their duty shirk

His wife and two children taken by flu
After he returned from the front
Just a locket left of all he knew
All other family dead or absent

Back here in the eighties people didn't care
How many died for country and king
There was striking and discord everywhere
They didn't owe these brave men a thing

The old man drifted into unconsciousness
Hypothermia was setting in fast
He finally slipped out of his battledress
And the old soldier breathed his last

So, lest we forget, wear your poppy with pride
For those men who gave lives without fear
Remember those who for freedom died
And remember those still here!!!

This is a true story of Private Henry Tandy who was a war hero and highly decorated, he - unbeknown at the time- spared Hitler his life at the end of WW1, he suffered for years after.

Hitler, What could have been.

Prologue:

By the crossroads at Menin in nineteen eighteen
An act of compassion, which was rarely seen
Saw a British Tommy spare a German life
Though the war was now over, killing was rife.

Henry Tandey was the Tommy who spared that man
His enemy was wounded, his face tired and wan
Henry raised his rifle but he just could not shoot
That soldier was Hitler, a fact none would dispute.

Private Henry Tandey:

How he won his medals

The most decorated private in World War one
Won the Military medal fighting the Hun
The Distinguished Conduct Medal for bravery
Yet was later chastised for setting Hitler free.

At a nearby French village conditions were dire
His regiment pinned down by machine gun fire
Henry crawled forward, stormed the nest - took it out
Led a bayonet charge causing enemy to rout.

Carrying wounded comrades to the first aid bay
Dodging enemy bullets in the last affray
Moving further forward they came upon a bridge
The enemy had shelled it caused lots of damage.

With a hole in the bridge, they thought that all was lost
He restored the planks, earned the Victoria cross
Under very heavy fire he got the job done
Henry kept on battling till the fight was well won.

Hitler and Neville Chamberlain:

Twenty years forward a historical greeting
Chamberlain shook hands with Hitler on their meeting
A painting was hung in the place where they met
Hitler had bought it so he would never forget.

The humanity of the soldier who let him live
That encounter with a man who tried to forgive
While smoking their cigars and drinking best brandy
Hitler pointed out the soldier Henry Tandey.

He said 'That man came close to killing me
I thought I'd never see my beloved Germany,
Please convey my respects when you go back,
Thank him for his forgiveness during that attack'

The consequences:

Chamberlain, returning was really in his prime
Waving worthless paper, it was peace in our time
But did he ring Henry? the records don't show
Living family members say 'yes it was so'

He told a reporter around nineteen forty
'If only I had known what he'd turn out to be,
Having seen the hatred he would nurture and grow,
I was so sorry to God to have let him go'

He existed the rest of his life tormented
Always aware of what he could have prevented
He tried to sign up at the age of forty nine
Tried to ensure Hitler didn't get away this time.

His death in 1977:

At Marcoing with his comrades, Henry was interred
Where most of the fighting initially occurred
Now finally free of blame in that sacred place
Just the scars of regret remain etched on his face.

Perhaps the most famous and most visited interment in history, no-one knows or will ever know the true identity of the soldier buried in Westminster Abbey among Kings of England.

The tomb of the Unknown Soldier

From the war torn battlefields,
Where the poppies abundant grew,
This bloody soil, a body yields,
What of his name? There's none that knew.

A Father's lad, a Mother's son,
Someone's Nephew, someone's Niece,
A Brother who is known to none,
Carried back home, to be at peace.

For him no more, the cannon rings,
The sound of guns, the sound of war,
For he shall lie among the kings,
Where guns are silent evermore.

That he should lie alone in peace,
Known just to God, and God alone,
Ne'er more to carry his valise,
Ne'er more an army's stepping stone.

To be entombed in this great church,
Beneath our Lords own imagery,
Will mean no mother has to search,
For laying here, her son could be.

The soldier from his mother's womb,
Where once he fought for freedom too,
Was placed into the empty tomb,
Back to darkness, to start anew.

The Lord did open Heaven's door,
Thus from his duties he'll dismiss,
This warrior who gave life and more,
Greater love, hath no man than this.

The war to end all wars did not!
For wars and killing still increase,
The bodies on war fields do rot,
Whilst Unknown soldier rests in peace.

This is my take of the jubilation felt by our families when war was declared in 1914, hunger was rife and work was rare, so war was welcomed, by closing the curtains I mean closing their eyes, the verses to me depict the aftermath and what I think would have been the feelings of most of those families.

Close all the curtains.

Close all the curtains, don't let them see
what has become of you and of me,
Let those confounded battle winds blow
let all those hot embers continue to glow,
Let men blow their bugles over our head
blast out the last post – for our glorious dead.

Those tired marching boots stirring the dust
of old memories and a long lost trust,
Those sons of mothers – marching along
escorted by a heavenly throng,
Climbing those stairs to be with their God
following where their ancestors trod.

So, draw those curtains, let no-one look in
at these deathly corpses, so young – so thin,
They walk cratered roads, these selfless dead
the same roads where living fear to tread,
Wait! Open those curtains, bring us more war
isn't war what we wanted? - then who could ask more.

Edith Louisa Cavell 4 December 1865 – 12 October 1915) was a British nurse. She is celebrated for saving the lives of soldiers from both sides without discrimination and in helping some 200 allied soldiers escape from German-occupied Belgium during WW1, for which she was arrested. She was accused of treason, found guilty by a Court martial and sentenced to death. Despite international pressure for mercy, she was shot by a German firing squad.

Edith Cavell.

Childhood:

In the year of our Lord eighteen sixty five,
On a depressingly cold, dark winter's morn,
Edith Louisa did finally arrive,
First child of Frederick and Louisa was born.

Her Father a reverend, taught her at home,
alongside siblings, Florence, Lillian and John.
Saturdays in Norfolk young Edith would roam,
on Sunday morning, she sat for Dad's sermon.

Although very strict, Edith's childhood was fun,
At eighteen a teacher, with excellent French,
A governess by the time she was twenty one,
As work came along, stepped up to the bench.

Training:

She was left a small legacy, traveled abroad,
Went to Austria and Bavaria where she met,
with Doctor Wolfenberg, and became overawed,
He ran a hospital, she helped with his debt.

This was the time nursing entered her mind,
she became interested in learning much more,
Over the next six years Edith would find,
Nursing was what she was put on earth for.

At Fountains fever hospital, time was spent,
appraising, if as a nurse she'd be suited,
To those training it was quite evident,
that in nursing her life was deep rooted.

A typhoid epidemic broke out in Kent,
Edith took along five nurses to assist,
Of almost two thousand, the great compliment,
there were less than two hundred died on the list.

Awarded a medal for her dedication,
For the next fifteen years, nursed the sick and the ailing,
Devoting her life to the health of a nation,
Her own life into insignificance paling.

Abroad:

Work took her to Brussels for over five years,
As governess for the family Francois,
Their jokes of Victoria, made her shed tears,
as she later revealed in her own memoirs.

In nineteen o seven, Edith pioneered,
training of nurses in Brussels outskirts,
Her ideas were welcomed, her views revered,
in a few short years she was training converts.

In Norfolk with her mother when war began,
Germany had invaded her second home,
With no fear for life, back to Belgium she ran,
even though over countryside, enemy did roam.

She sent home the Dutch nurses, German ones too,
told the rest their duty was to nurse and care,

despite nationality, all they could do,
was tend to the wounded and those in despair.

Enemy advance was swift, Brits retreated,
along with the French, a lot of them cut off,
In just a few weeks both armies defeated,
Lines of communication quickly shut off.

Two British soldiers made their way to her school,
she sheltered them safely for over two weeks,
She knew it meant death, she was nobody's fool,
Kept it to herself, in case there were leaks.

They soon established an underground lifeline,
Masterminded by Prince and Princess De Croy,
Though no one could afford to be asinine,
In the Red Cross hospital rules didn't apply.

Capture:

Just one year later, two escape members were caught,
Edith was arrested and warned they'd told all,
In her naivety, although she'd been fraught,
she'd confessed everything before nightfall.

She'd trusted her captors and made a clean breast,
trained to protect life not throw it away,
Under German court she was put to the test,
Found guilty and therefore must die the next day.

Her words:

I realise that patriotism isn't enough,
I have no hatred or bitterness to share,
I do not believe, I've been treated rough,
I go to my God with no tears to spare.

I've no fear nor shrinking, I've seen death,
so often that it is no stranger to me,
I think of my good life, before my last breath,
As I stand in view of God and eternity.

Death:

They took her outside the following day,
Frog marched her to their own rifle range,
But one German soldier refused right away,
His officer calling him a coward and deranged.

The officer pulled out his pistol and fired,
Into the kneeling soldier's head point blank.

Shouted to the others that he was undesired,
Scared squad fired at Edith, to floor she sank.

The Outcome:

Germans were shocked at the following outcry,
Knew they'd committed a worldwide scandal,
There was no way that they could justify,
The murder was more than nations could handle.

Over two hundred soldiers had made it back,
Thanks to Edith and her underground friends,
After the war, the authorities weren't slack,
They exhumed her remains, to make amends.

Her remains were carried with great celebration,
to Norfolk cathedral in a poignant scene,
Edith Cavell, whose heart touched a nation,
re-buried outside, in a spot called Life's Green.

This Woman driven by a sense of devotion,
and practical living of her own belief,
Laid to rest at last, with simplistic emotion,
Much to her family's grateful relief

-

---

*There are still ex soldiers living on our streets today, some choose to
live that way but some are simply living in poverty or need help.
With the advent of organisations like the British Legion and Help for
Heroes this has mostly stopped, but there is always someone in need
of help - this poem is set in the seventies.*

Medals of Honour?

I walked right past him on the street,
No shoes upon his dirty feet,
That spindly thin skeleton form,
Wrapped blankets round to keep him warm.

He held his hand out - begged for cash,
I caught a glimpse, just a quick flash,
Arrayed across a ragged vest,
A row of medals on his chest.

Why was he there..how could this be?
A man who fought for his country,
Forced onto streets no fixed abode,
Worldly belongings, 'neath him stowed.

Rich people with their shopping bags,
Rush by the soldier dressed in rags,
They walk right by, ignore his pleas,
Young children stop to taunt and tease.

I gave him cash, he took my hand,
'My friend, listen, please understand,
I chose this life for I have sinned,
Though medals on my chest are pinned.

I've gone to war, seen horrid things,
Seen what hate and greed can bring,
Seen old men weep and children killed,
Seen women raped, men's lust fulfilled.

Yet I don't suffer as they did,
Of suffering I am well rid,
I helped create this world of sin,
And now asked God to come within.

Forgive my sins for what I've done,
To trust me as he would his Son,
Who died for all - that we might live,
Each day I ask God to forgive;

I bared my soul for all to see,
These medals are nothing to me,
I regret the path that I have trod,
And soon will be with my true God'.

With that he rested..short of breath,
He surely was so close to death,
I called medics on nearby phone,
But he was gone, his spirit flown.

I looked above as he lay there,
And saw his spirit climb the stair,
May that man's war forever cease,
That he might find eternal peace.

His medals, now in a Museum,
Lots of children come to see them;
Yet the owner wanted nothing more,
Than an end to senseless war!

Moina Belle Michael (August 15, 1869 – May 10, 1944) was an American professor and humanitarian who conceived the idea of *using poppies as a rememberance flower for those who served in World War* 1.

MoinaMicheal.

'In Flanders field' by John McCrae,
is quoted on Remembrance day,
All about the poppy flower,
the symbolism, and the power
of those who gave their lives away.

Moina worked hard for the YMCA.
In New York city, worked all day,
In November nineteen eighteen,
One young soldier, spotless and clean.
dropped 'Ladies home Journal' in her tray.

She read a poem, 'We shall not sleep'
how poppies through the mud would creep,
and brave men who saw sunset glow,
dead in Flanders in ground below,
Reading on, she began to weep.

She read-----
Take up our quarrel with the foe,
To you from failing hands we throw,
The torch; be yours to hold it high,
If ye break faith with us who die,
We shall not sleep, though poppies grow
In Flanders field.

With handkerchief she dabbed her eye,
Read of the larks up in the sky,
In the air, still bravely singing,
toward crosses they were winging,
And then she sat, wrote this reply.

Her reply:
Oh you who sleep in Flanders field,
Sweet sleep - to rise anew,
We caught the torch you threw,
and holding high, we keep the faith,
with all who died.

Three delegates within the room,
while passing by, noted the gloom,
Paid ten dollars for the flowers,
"To make your day, as you made ours,
providing all those lovely blooms"

'I'll buy more blooms with this' she said,

'I'll buy them for those men who bled',
She showed the poem and her reply,
one man wiped a tear from his eye,
She left to find some poppies red.

She searched and searched then found her prize,
just twenty five to her surprise,
One very large, the others were small.
She carried them back to the hall,
and was surrounded by the guys.

'I'll take one' every man would say,
'I'll wear it with pride, every day,'
She gave them out, till all were gone,
then she remembered the large one,
in her buttonhole she displayed.

That was when her campaign began
to adopt the poppy for man,
recognise, they'd given their all,
fought for their country, heard its call
So Moinas campaign ran and ran.

The US Legion took on the cause,
To honor those home from the wars,
Nineteen twenty, the voting ran,
Every old soldier, every man,
took the poppy and opened doors.

So this November, don't avoid,
Remember those brave men who died,
Think of Moina who slaved for years,
Think of families who shed tears,
Wear your poppy, WEAR IT WITH PRIDE.

Lest we forget.

---

*John (Jack) Simpson Kirkpatrick (6 July 1892 – 19 May 1915), who
served under the name **John Simpson**, was a stretcher bearer with
the 1st Australian Division during the Gallipoli campaign in WW1.
After landing at Anzac cove on 25 April 1915, Simpson began to use
donkeysto provide first aid and carry wounded soldiers to the beach,
for evacuation. Simpson and the donkeys continued this work for
three and a half weeks, often under fire, until he was killed in the
third attack on Anzac cove. "**Simpson and his Donkey**" are a part of
the "Anzac legend".*

John Simpson Kirkpatrick.

Mortimer school was a long way away.
When Jack first stepped on Australian land,
Memories of donkeys and how they would bray,
Far away on South Shields golden sand.

Mr George paid him well through school holidays,
To give donkey rides down on the beach,
He remembered fondly those halcyon days,
Now far away and well out of reach.

He recalled his Mother stood at the door,
Hair immaculately tied in a bun,
Rolled up sleeves neath white pinafore,
Waving goodbye to her only son.

Jack enrolled as a stoker at seventeen,
On a vessel bound for New South Wales,
The ship was a wreck, should never have been,
allowed to sail through rough seas and gales.

That's how he found himself here on these shores,
Jumping ship just to save his own life,
But there in West Melbourne among the whores,
sickness and pestilence were rife.

He became very ill and went down with flu,
confined to bed for three weeks or more,
As he lay alone thought of homeland grew,
His heart called him back to England's shores.

Jack soon realised that life at sea was good,
and enrolled as a stoker once more,
But he returned to Perth as fast as he could,
hearing England and Germany were at war.

Once again he jumped ship and enlisted,
in the Australian Imperial Force,
On just two shillings a day he existed,
with four shillings sent home as resource.

Embarking from Freemantle they were sent
overseas to Egypt where they trained,
In the shadows of the Sphinx days were spent,
Nights were freezing but no one complained.

They were then shipped to Lemnos Island where
for weeks the Third Field Ambulance trained,
Jack registered his last will and testament there,
His old Mother the one to have gained.

In April due to unknown circumstance,
on the troopship Devanha they'd board,
To the Dardanelles the troops would advance,
every man knelt and prayed to the Lord.

Errors were made on the spot where they'd land,
they soon realised that things had gone wrong,
Hundreds of men lay dying on the sand,
Stretcher bearers worked all night long.

But the stretchers they used to carry the wounded,
Were not being returned to the shore,
The reasons for this left bearers dumbfounded,
how were they supposed to rescue more.

Jack single handedly carrying back men,
was about to lift another on his back,
He was looking around him that was when,
he saw an abandoned donkey on the track.

He lifted the wounded man onto it's back,
and the legend of Jack Simpson was born,
News spread fast about the donkey and Jack,
though on his actions officers poured scorn.

After four long days away from his unit,
he was a deserter in the army's eye,
Men knew of his bravery, his true grit,
sightings of Jack in the field didn't belie.

With the donkey he worked an eighteen hour day,
taking water to the men in their trench,
Carrying wounded men back from the fray,
away from the madness and the stench.

Duffy the donkey and Jack became known,
among the Diggers in the Monash Valley,
They said he had guts, a strong backbone,
when he was about, the men would rally.

Though warned about snipers time after time,
his whistling and singing was heard,
by those men in the trenches covered in grime,
as the cries of the wounded were answered.

Up through Shrapnel Gully which was the route
to Monash valley and the main front line,
past Dead man's Ridge where snipers would shoot,
yet their confidence Jack would undermine.

Leaving the donkey hidden from harm,

Jack collected the injured alone,
Taking his chance while things were calm,
toting them back to the safety zone.

Jack's luck was never going to last,
he was killed by machine gun fire,
just twenty four days in Turkey had passed,
that brave Geordie was freed from the mire.

So there, in Shrapnel Valley he lay,
the man with the donkey had done his part,
all his comrades would kneel and would pray
on the beach at Hell Spit where he gave his heart.

A simple wooden cross marked the spot,
of this medic who gave all he could give,
at only twenty two his own life he gave,
in order that fellow Anzacs could live.

Yet no recognition, no Victoria cross,
despite recommendations, letters and pleas,
The British army just didn't give a toss,
they had no understanding, no empathy!

---

*A little boy is walking holding his Mother's hand in an occupied
country in WW1, they pass a German soldier and the boy stares long
and hard at him-*

Mutual hatred.

Soldier.

Why do you stare so little boy?
Turn back your head and don't annoy!
Go, walk away, hold mother's hand
When you're a man, you'll understand.
About these things, how war must be
Why we must fight – your dad and me,
Go on your way and watch your tongue
I will not fight with one so young.

Boy.

I stare because you stare at me,
Hate in your eyes I clearly see,
When I am tall I'll fight you too!
I'll take my bayonet – run you through.
To quiet towns like mine you come

Too scared to fight upon the Somme,
So go you coward hold your tongue
For one day I'll not be so young!

---

*I went Ypres a few years ago and visited the War cemeteries there -
both Allied and German - it inspired me to write this poem.*

Rows of White Crosses.

The poppy grows where many have died,
Tis watered by the tears they cried,
Swathes of poppies, a thousand miles wide,
Grow from souls of those valiant men,
The likes of which we won't see again.

Rusting enfields pierce ground of mud,
Dead man's helmet where he last stood,
Fighting the enemy, gave his blood,
Those brave young souls, those selfless men
The likes of which we won't see again.

Fields of white crosses all in a row,
Where thousands of wild poppies would grow,
Immaculate, for those men below,
We thought we had lost all those brave men,
But twenty years later we'd see them again.

---

*This poem was inspired by an old soldier at a war memoriam, the
shadow he casts is that of a modern soldier with gun in hand, a very
moving image.*

The Memorial.

Outside the cold grey slab of stone,
Where friends once stood, he stands alone,
His frame now bent, stick at his side,
Yet tall he stands - face full of pride,
His war long over, his freedom won,
He stands alone, old friends long gone.

The shadow cast of recent time,
And wars fought now as church bells chime,
The soldier poised with gun in hand,
Waits silently for his command,

And guards the old man standing proud,
As bugler plays 'Last Post' aloud.

Not much between them through the years,
For they've both fought and shed their tears,
The shadow falls on men who died,
Where mason carved their names with pride,
Both fought for what they thought was true,
But, who stands in the shadow of who?

---

*Robert Gordon McBeath, VC(22 December 1898 – 9 October 1922)
was a Scottish recipient of the Victoria Cross, the highest and most
prestigious medal that can be awarded to members of British
military forces. Following the end of World War I McBeath married
and emigrated to Canada where he was killed in the line of duty
while working as a police officer in Vancouver British Columbia, this
is his true heroic story -*

Robert McBeath VC

Robert Gordon McBeath was raised
and adopted by a sister and brother,
Through school he was always well praised
and although without father or mother
throughout childhood was never fazed,
nor was he concerned about any other.

'Eighteen years' the young man cried
as the Sergeant asked him his age,
The soldier knew the boy had lied
through past experience he could gauge,
His own law of reason he applied
and history turned another page.

Although the lad looked just sixteen
the recruiting Sergeant saw a trait,
He could see the boy was very keen
and with his fervour could relate
for enthusiasm rarely seen
he knew the lad wouldn't deviate.

So the Seaforth Highlanders he joined
reviewed by the Duke of Sutherland,
Prior to going where they were assigned
he promised survivors a piece of croftland,
But for a VC winner a farm was consigned
for those returning heroes in Scotland.

Then off to war in France he went
a Veteran by nineteen seventeen,
There on the Somme his time was spent
at the tender age of just nineteen,
On staying alive he was hellbent
although the Hun tried to intervene.

So in the very first battles
involving British massed tanks,
The German army was rattled
as they scattered their ranks,
forced to leave all their chattels
in those vile trenches so dank.

A German counter-attack next day
recovered the ground they had lost,
The enemy made an impressive display
as the British found out to their cost,
Machine gun nests causing disarray
hand grenades being freely tossed.

Pinned down by the intense gunfire
Lance Corporal McBeath volunteered,
With a Lewis gun he did aspire
and toward the enemy he veered,
Firing his gun through the quagmire
as one by one each nest he cleared,

Enemy soldiers under attack
ran into a safe tunnel nearby,
Mac was mad allowed them no slack
slid into the tunnel whereby
men down there were taken aback
they all surrendered rather than die!

He captured them all as one lot
took thirty three men from the chaos,
They rose from the dark, one man shot,
all were fed up having to doss
in the hell of that terrible spot,
For this he won the Victoria cross.

Surviving war he went home to wed
his sweetheart Barbara Mackay,

He claimed his farm as the Duke had said
but sold it, there he couldn't stay,
leaving the place they were born and bred
to Vancouver they made their way.

Joining the British Columbia police
they settled in Vancouver city,
He wasn't happy, wanted quick release
they needed more cash in the Kitty,
He then joined the Vancouver police
where the work was tough and gritty.

It was then in nineteen twenty two
with partner Detective R Quirk,
On Granville and Davie there was a to-do
and duty they never would shirk,
They stood in the road, told the driver to
pull over, but he was a jerk.

Both jumped onto the running board
of the car driven by Fred Deal,
On down the street the old car roared
almost dragging them under the wheel,
it finally stopped as they implored
grinding to a halt with a roar.

Marjorie Earl was also in the car
Quirk remained to watch over her,
Watching McBeath and Deal from afar
as a gun was pulled causing a stir,
The two men desperately started to spar
Quirk saw a flash, the rest was a blur.

Quirk quickly raced over to his aid
a flash, a bullet, through his hand,
although in danger, he wasn't afraid
but things didn't go as he planned,
another shot and McBeath swayed
as Deal made his final stand.

Deal fired again as he ran away
striking Quirk on the side of his head,
Should he give chase, or should he stay
the pavement was already bright red,
Staying with McBeath he began to pray
though his friend was already dead.

The suspect's face was flashed around
he was safe till a witness sang,
Police raced to where he'd gone to ground
he admitted causing the whole shebang,

Of attempted murder he was found
guilty of murder, sentenced to hang.

McBeath's funeral was the biggest seen
as shops and Banks closed their doors,
for the biggest hero that's ever been
and ever set foot on Canada's shores,
Thousands attended the poignant scene
passing shuttered windows, shuttered doors.

Things weren't so bad for murderer Deal
his conviction was now overturned,
Found guilty of manslaughter after appeal,
never got the death sentence earned,
Robert's wife was homesick, life was unreal
back to Scotland Barbara returned.

---

*This is the final poem in this my first ever book, I hope you have
enjoyed the poems and that they may help to explain what those
brave men from all walks of life and from all over the world suffered,
I have deliberately left this poem till last, for me it just about sums
up what every Mother must have thought during this terrible war,
thank you for reading and God bless.*

The Telegram.

Alone she sits in dressing gown,
her world around her falling down,
The crumpled telegram in hand,
The words so blurred, so harsh, so bland.

The day had started really well,
The war was over so they tell,
In battlefields no more he'd roam,
In six weeks' time he'd be back home.

Back home to sit in pastures green,
To hold the boy he'd never seen,
Now four years old, running around,
Not for him that merry-go round--

-Of war, destruction, living hell
He wouldn't hear the bell's death knell,
The paper signed by foreign power,
Eleventh day, eleventh hour.

Then came the rap upon her door,
Her bones they shivered to the core,

Her legs went weak, had no control,
All hope gone from her empty soul.

He stood there quietly, alone,
That skinny boy, so barely grown,
Gave her the paper avoided her eye,
She opened it, cried 'No reply'

The words resounded in her head,
They've made a mistake, he can't be dead,
She read the name, Private Ian Pound,
Missing in action on foreign ground.

Despite her prayers he never returned,
Advances of suitors rejected, spurned,
Her heart knew no other, first true love,
Fitting together like hand in glove.

She raised her son to be a man,
He went off to war, was killed at Cannes,
A telegram once more received,
Another loved one to be grieved.

With bitter heart she struggled on,
In the shadow of World War one
and World War two, she lived her life,
Full of sorrow and full of strife.

Today she sits there, old and grand,
Two crumpled papers in her hand,
The telegrams of both her men,
She closed her eyes, joined them again.

I leave the final word to that wonderful poet Robert Laurence Binyon
They shall grow not old, as we that are left grow old:
Age shall not weary them, nor the years condemn.
At the going down of the sun and in the morning
We will remember them.

28891519R00026